Brielle, big helper

by Esther Slade

Illustrated by Marianella Aguirre
Edited by Isabella St Hilaire

Copyright © 2013 by Esther Slade

All rights reserved.

ISBN: 149220188X
ISBN-13: 978-1492201885
LCCN: 2013915630

dedication
for Isabella and Brielle

Brielle lives at home with her mom, dad, sister and grandma.
Brielle loves to help her family.

Brielle loves to go shopping with her mom.

When her mom comes home from the store,

Brielle helps her carry the bags.

Brielle loves to help her mom at dinner time!

When it is time for dinner,

Brielle helps her mom set the table.

When dinner is over,

Brielle helps her mom

clean up and dry the dishes.

Brielle loves her grandma Mae very much.

When her grandma wants to read,

Brielle helps her finds her glasses.

When her grandma is ready for bed,
Brielle turns the light off for her.

Brielle's best friend is her sister Bella.
When her sister is finished playing with her toys,
Brielle helps her put them away in the toy box.

Brielle loves to help her sister Bella.

When her sister Bella plays the piano,

Brielle cheers for her and says "bravo, bravo."

When Brielle walks with her

sister Bella to school,

she helps her carry her books.

Brielle loves helping her Dad!

When the trash can is full,

Brielle helps him take the trash out.

When her dad is in the driveway fixing his truck, Brielle hands him the tools.

Brielle loves helping her family.

She is a big helper.

The End.

About The Author

Esther Slade was born on the island of St. Thomas in the US Virgin Islands. Her formative years were spent on the islands of St. Croix and Antigua. Esther has an undergraduate degree in English from Temple University and a graduate degree from the University of Connecticut in Storrs, CT. Esther Slade is the author of Ayla's Paradise, J'ouvert Morning, Tithe of Blood and Mae, Drucilla and Ilene: Stories of These and Other Caribbean Women. She currently resides on the US Mainland with her two precious daughters, Bella and Brielle.

Made in United States
Orlando, FL
02 May 2022